Louisa Pallant

Henry James

Contents

LOUISA PALLANT

BY

Henry James

I

Never say you know the last words about any human heart! I was once treated to a revelation which startled and touched me in the nature of a person with whom I had been acquainted--well, as I supposed--for years, whose character I had had good reasons, heaven knows, to appreciate and in regard to whom I flattered myself I had nothing more to learn.

It was on the terrace of the Kursaal at Homburg, nearly ten years ago, one beautiful night toward the end of July. I had come to the place that day from Frankfort, with vague intentions, and was mainly occupied in waiting for my young nephew, the only son of my sister, who had been entrusted to my care by a very fond mother for the summer--I was expected to show him Europe, only the very best of it--and was on his way from Paris to join me. The excellent band discoursed music not too abstruse, while the air was filled besides with the murmur of different languages, the smoke of many cigars, the creak on the gravel of the gardens of strolling shoes and the thick tinkle of beer-glasses. There were a hundred people walking about, there were some in clusters at little tables and many on benches and rows of chairs, watching the others as if they had paid for the privilege and were rather disappointed. I was among these last; I sat by myself, smoking my cigar and thinking of nothing very particular while families and couples passed and repassed me.

I scarce know how long I had sat when I became aware of a recognition which made my meditations definite. It was on my own part, and the object of it was a lady who moved to and fro, unconscious of my observation, with a young girl at her side. I hadn't seen her for ten years, and what first struck me was the fact not that she was Mrs. Henry Pallant, but that the girl who was with her was remarkably pretty--or rather first of all that every one who passed appeared extremely to admire. This led me also to notice the young lady myself, and her charming face diverted my attention for some time from that of her companion. The latter, moreover, though it was night, wore a thin light veil which made her features vague. The couple slowly walked and walked, but though they were very quiet and decorous, and also very well dressed, they seemed to have no friends. Every one observed but no one addressed them; they appeared even themselves to exchange very few words. Moreover they bore with marked composure and as if they were thoroughly used to it the attention they excited. I am afraid it occurred to me to take for granted that they were of an artful intention and that if they hadn't been the elder lady would have handed the younger over a little less to public valuation and not have sought so to conceal her own face. Perhaps this question came into my mind too easily just then--in view of my prospective mentorship to my nephew. If I was to show him only the best of Europe I should have to be very careful about the people he should meet--especially the ladies--and the relations he should form. I suspected him of great innocence and was uneasy about my office. Was I completely relieved and reassured when I became aware that I simply had Louisa Pallant before me and that the girl was her daughter Linda, whom I had known as a child--Linda grown up to charming beauty?

The question was delicate and the proof that I was not very sure is perhaps that I forbore to speak to my pair at once. I watched them a while--I wondered what they would do. No great harm assuredly; but I was anxious to see if they were really isolated. Homburg was then a great resort of the English--the London season took up its tale there toward the first of August--and I had an idea that in such a company as that Louisa would naturally know people. It was my impression that she "cultivated" the English, that she had been much in London and would be likely to have views in regard to a permanent settlement there. This supposition was quickened by the sight of Linda's beauty, for I knew there is no country in which such attractions are more appreciated. You will see what time I took, and I confess that as I finished my cigar I thought it all over. There was no good reason in fact why I should have rushed into Mrs. Pallant's arms. She had not treated me well and we had never really made it up. Somehow even the circumstance that--after the first soreness--I was glad to have lost her had never put us quite right with each other; nor, for herself, had it made her less ashamed of her heartless behaviour that poor Pallant proved finally no great catch. I had forgiven her; I hadn't felt it anything but an escape not to have married a girl who had in her to take back her given word and break a fellow's heart for mere flesh-pots--or the shallow promise, as it pitifully turned out, of flesh-pots. Moreover we had met since then--on the occasion of my former visit to Europe; had looked each other in the eyes, had pretended to be easy friends and had talked of the wickedness of the world as composedly as if we were the only just, the only pure. I knew by that time what she had given out--that I had driven her off by my insane jealousy before she ever thought of Henry Pallant, before she had ever seen him. This hadn't been before and couldn't be to-day a ground of real reunion, especially if you add to it that she knew perfectly what I thought of her. It seldom ministers to friendship, I believe, that your friend shall know your real opinion, for he knows it mainly when it's unfavourable, and this is especially the case if--let the solecism pass!--he be a woman. I hadn't followed Mrs. Pallant's fortunes; the years went by for me in my own country, whereas she led her life, which I vaguely believed to be difficult after her husband's death--virtually that of a bankrupt--in foreign lands. I heard of her from time to time; always as "established" somewhere, but on each occasion in a different place. She drifted from country to country, and if she had been of a hard composition at the beginning it could never occur to me that her struggle with society, as it might be called, would have softened the paste. Whenever I heard a woman spoken of as "horribly worldly" I thought immediately of the object of my early passion. I imagined she had debts, and when I now at last made up my mind to recall myself to her it was present to me that she might ask me to lend her money. More than anything else, however, at this time of day, I was sorry for her, so that such an idea didn't operate as a deterrent.

She pretended afterwards that she hadn't noticed me--expressing as we stood face to face great surprise and wishing to know where I had dropped from; but I think the corner of her eye had taken me in and she had been waiting to see what I would do. She had ended by sitting down with her girl on the same row of chairs with myself, and after a little, the seat next to her becoming vacant, I had gone and stood before her. She had then looked up at me a moment, staring as if she couldn't imagine who I was or what I wanted; after which, smiling and extending her hands, she had broken out: "Ah my dear old friend--what a delight!" If she had waited to see what I would do in order to choose her own line she thus at least carried out this line with the utmost grace. She was cordial, friendly, artless, interested, and indeed I'm sure she was very glad to see me. I may as well say immediately, none the less, that she gave me neither then nor later any sign of a desire to contract a loan. She had scant means--that I learned--yet seemed for the moment able to pay her way. I took the empty chair and we remained in talk for an hour. After a while she made me sit at her other side, next her daughter, whom she wished to know me--to love me--as one of their oldest friends. "It goes back, back, back, doesn't it?" said Mrs. Pallant; "and of course she remembers you as a child." Linda smiled all sweetly and blankly, and I saw she remembered me not a whit. When her mother threw out that they had often talked about me she failed to take it up, though she looked extremely nice. Looking nice was her strong point; she was prettier even than her mother had been. She was such a little lady that she made me ashamed of having doubted, however vaguely and for a moment, of her position in the scale of propriety. Her appearance seemed to say that if she had no acquaintances it was because she didn't want them--because nobody there struck her as attractive: there wasn't the slightest difficulty about her choosing her friends. Linda Pallant, young as she was, and fresh and fair and charming, gentle and sufficiently shy, looked somehow exclusive--as if the dust of the common world had never been meant to besprinkle her. She was of thinner consistency than her mother and clearly not a young woman of professions--except in so far as she was committed to an interest in you by her bright pure candid smile. No girl who had such a lovely way of parting her lips could pass for designing.

As I sat between the pair I felt I had been taken possession of and that for better or worse my stay at Homburg would be intimately associated with theirs. We gave each other a great deal of news and expressed unlimited interest in each other's history since our last meeting. I mightn't judge of what Mrs. Pallant kept back, but for myself I quite overflowed. She let me see at any rate that her life had been a good deal what I supposed, though the terms she employed to describe it were less crude than those of my thought. She confessed they had drifted, she and her daughter, and were drifting still. Her narrative rambled and took a wrong turn, a false flight, or two, as I thought Linda noted, while she sat watching the passers, in a manner that betrayed no consciousness of their attention, without coming to her mother's aid. Once or twice Mrs. Pallant made me rather feel a cross-questioner, which I had had no intention of being. I took it that if the girl never put in a word it was because she had perfect confidence in her parent's ability to come out straight. It was suggested to me, I scarcely knew how, that this confidence between the two ladies went to a great length; that their union of thought, their system of reciprocal divination, was remarkable, and that they probably seldom needed to resort to the clumsy and in some cases dangerous expedient of communicating by sound. I suppose I made this reflexion not all at once--it was not wholly the result of that first meeting. I was with them constantly for the next several days and my impressions had time to clarify.

I do remember, however, that it was on this first evening that Archie's name came up. She attributed her own stay at Homburg to no refined nor exalted motive--didn't put it that she was there from force of habit or because a high medical authority had ordered her to drink the waters; she frankly admitted the reason of her visit to have been simply that she didn't know where else to turn. But she appeared to assume that my behaviour rested on higher grounds and even that it required explanation, the place being frivolous and modern--devoid of that interest of antiquity which I had ever made so much of. "Don't you remember--ever so long ago--that you wouldn't look at anything in Europe that wasn't a thousand years old? Well, as we advance in life I suppose we don't think that quite such a charm." And when I mentioned that I had arrived because the place was as good as another for awaiting my nephew she exclaimed: "Your nephew--what nephew? He must have come up of late." I answered that his name was Archie Parker and that he was modern indeed; he was to attain legal manhood in a few months and was in Europe for the first time. My last news of him had been from Paris and I was expecting to hear further from one day to the other. His father was dead, and though a selfish bachelor, little versed in the care of children, I was considerably counted on by his mother to see that he didn't smoke nor flirt too much, nor yet tumble off an Alp.

Mrs. Pallant immediately guessed that his mother was my sister Charlotte, whom she spoke of familiarly, though I knew she had scarce seen her. Then in a moment it came to her which of the Parkers Charlotte had married; she remembered the family perfectly from the old New York days--"that disgustingly rich set." She said it was very nice having the boy come out that way to my care; to which I replied that it was very nice for the boy. She pronounced the advantage rather mine--I ought to have had children; there was something so parental about me and

I would have brought them up so well. She could make an allusion like that--to all that might have been and had not been--without a gleam of guilt in her eye; and I foresaw that before I left the place I should have confided to her that though I detested her and was very glad we had fallen out, yet our old relations had left me no heart for marrying another woman. If I had remained so single and so sterile the fault was nobody's but hers. She asked what I meant to do with my nephew--to which I replied that it was much more a question of what he would do with me. She wished to know if he were a nice young man and had brothers and sisters and any particular profession. I assured her I had really seen little of him; I believed him to be six feet high and of tolerable parts. He was an only son, but there was a little sister at home, a delicate, rather blighted child, demanding all the mother's care.

"So that makes your responsibility greater, as it were, about the boy, doesn't it?" said Mrs. Pallant.

"Greater? I'm sure I don't know."

"Why if the girl's life's uncertain he may become, some moment, all the mother has. So that being in your hands--"

"Oh I shall keep him alive, I suppose, if you mean that," I returned.

"Well, WE won't kill him, shall we, Linda?" my friend went on with a laugh.

"I don't know--perhaps we shall!" smiled the girl.

II

I called on them the next at their lodgings, the modesty of which was enhanced by a hundred pretty feminine devices--flowers and photographs and portable knick-knacks and a hired piano and morsels of old brocade flung over angular sofas. I took them to drive; I met them again at the Kursaal; I arranged that we should dine together, after the Homburg fashion, at the same table d'hote; and during several days this revived familiar intercourse continued, imitating intimacy if not quite achieving it. I was pleased, as my companions passed the time for me and the conditions of our life were soothing--the feeling of summer and shade and music and leisure in the German gardens and woods, where we strolled and sat and gossiped; to which may be added a vague sociable sense that among people whose challenge to the curiosity was mainly not irresistible we kept quite to ourselves. We were on the footing of old friends who still had in regard to each other discoveries to make. We knew each other's nature but didn't know each other's experience; so that when Mrs. Pallant related to me what she had been "up to," as I called it, for so many years, the former knowledge attached a hundred interpretative footnotes--as if I had been editing an author who presented difficulties--to the interesting page. There was nothing new to me in the fact that I didn't esteem her, but there was relief in my finding that this wasn't necessary at Homburg and that I could like her in spite of it. She struck me, in the oddest way, as both improved and degenerate; the two processes, in her nature, might have gone on together. She was battered and world-worn and, spiritually speaking, vulgarised; something fresh had rubbed off her--it even included the vivacity of her early desire to do the best thing for herself--and something rather stale had rubbed on. At the same time she betrayed a scepticism, and that was rather becoming, for it had quenched the eagerness of her prime, the mercenary principle I had so suffered from. She had grown weary and detached, and since she affected me as more impressed with the evil of the world than with the good, this was a gain; in other words her accretion of indifference, if not of cynicism, showed a softer surface than that of her old ambitions. Furthermore I had to recognise that her devotion to her daughter was a kind of religion; she had done the very best possible for Linda.

Linda was curious, Linda was interesting; I've seen girls I liked better--charming as this one might be--but have never seen one who for the hour you were with her (the impression passed somehow when she was out of sight) occupied you so completely. I can best describe the attention she provoked by saying that she struck you above all things as a felicitous FINAL product--after the fashion of some plant or some fruit, some waxen orchid or some perfect peach. She was clearly the result of a process of calculation, a process patiently educative, a pressure exerted, and all artfully, so that she should reach a high point.

This high point had been the star of her mother's heaven--it hung before her so unquenchably--and had shed the only light (in default of a better) that was to shine on the poor lady's path. It stood her instead of every other ideal. The very most and the very best--that was what the girl had been led on to achieve; I mean of course, since no real miracle had been wrought, the most and the best she was capable of. She was as pretty, as graceful, as intelligent, as well-bred, as well-informed, as well-dressed, as could have been conceived for her; her music, her singing, her German, her French, her English, her step, her tone, her glance, her manner, everything in her person and movement, from the shade and twist of her hair to the way you saw her finger-nails were pink when she raised her hand, had been carried so far that one found one's self accepting them as the very measure of young grace. I regarded her thus as a model, yet it was a part of her perfection that she had none of the stiffness of a pattern. If she held the observation it was because you wondered where and when she would break down; but she never broke down, either in her French accent or in her role of educated angel.

After Archie had come the ladies were manifestly his greatest resource, and all the world knows why a party of four is more convenient than a party of three. My nephew had kept me waiting a week, with a serenity all his own; but this very coolness was a help to harmony--so long, that is, as I didn't lose my temper with it. I didn't, for the most part, because my young man's unperturbed acceptance of the

most various forms of good fortune had more than anything else the effect of amus-
ing me. I had seen little of him for the last three or four years; I wondered what his
impending majority would have made of him--he didn't at all carry himself as if the
wind of his fortune were rising--and I watched him with a solicitude that usually
ended in a joke. He was a tall fresh-coloured youth, with a candid circular coun-
tenance and a love of cigarettes, horses and boats which had not been sacrificed to
more strenuous studies. He was reassuringly natural, in a supercivilised age, and I
soon made up my mind that the formula of his character was in the clearing of the
inward scene by his so preordained lack of imagination. If he was serene this was
still further simplifying. After that I had time to meditate on the line that divides
the serene from the inane, the simple from the silly. He wasn't clever; the fonder
theory quite defied our cultivation, though Mrs. Pallant tried it once or twice; but
on the other hand it struck me his want of wit might be a good defensive weapon.
It wasn't the sort of density that would let him in, but the sort that would keep him
out. By which I don't mean that he had shortsighted suspicions, but that on the
contrary imagination would never be needed to save him, since she would never
put him in danger. He was in short a well-grown well-washed muscular young
American, whose extreme salubrity might have made him pass for conceited. If he
looked pleased with himself it was only because he was pleased with life--as well
he might be, with the fortune that awaited the stroke of his twenty-first year--and
his big healthy independent person was an inevitable part of that. I am bound to
add that he was accommodating--for which I was grateful. His habits were active,
but he didn't insist on my adopting them and he made numerous and generous sac-
rifices for my society. When I say he made them for mine I must duly remember
that mine and that of Mrs. Pallant and Linda were now very much the same thing.
He was willing to sit and smoke for hours under the trees or, adapting his long
legs to the pace of his three companions, stroll through the nearer woods of the
charming little hill-range of the Taunus to those rustic Wirthschaften where coffee
might be drunk under a trellis. Mrs. Pallant took a great interest in him; she made
him, with his easy uncle, a subject of discourse; she pronounced him a delightful
specimen, as a young gentleman of his period and country. She even asked me the
sort of "figure" his fortune might really amount to, and professed a rage of envy
when I told her what I supposed it to be. While we were so occupied Archie, on his

side, couldn't do less than converse with Linda, nor to tell the truth did he betray the least inclination for any different exercise. They strolled away together while their elders rested; two or three times, in the evening, when the ballroom of the Kursaal was lighted and dance-music played, they whirled over the smooth floor in a waltz that stirred my memory. Whether it had the same effect on Mrs. Pallant's I know not: she held her peace. We had on certain occasions our moments, almost our half-hours, of unembarrassed silence while our young companions disported themselves. But if at other times her enquiries and comments were numerous on this article of my ingenuous charge, that might very well have passed for a courteous recognition of the frequent admiration I expressed for Linda--an admiration that drew from her, I noticed, but scant direct response. I was struck thus with her reserve when I spoke of her daughter--my remarks produced so little of a maternal flutter. Her detachment, her air of having no fatuous illusions and not being blinded by prejudice, seemed to me at times to savour of affectation. Either she answered me with a vague and impatient sigh and changed the subject, or else she said before doing so: "Oh yes, yes, she's a very brilliant creature. She ought to be: God knows what I've done for her!" The reader will have noted my fondness, in all cases, for the explanations of things; as an example of which I had my theory here that she was disappointed in the girl. Where then had her special calculation failed? As she couldn't possibly have wished her prettier or more pleasing, the pang must have been for her not having made a successful use of her gifts. Had she expected her to "land" a prince the day after leaving the schoolroom? There was after all plenty of time for this, with Linda but two-and-twenty. It didn't occur to me to wonder if the source of her mother's tepidity was that the young lady had not turned out so nice a nature as she had hoped, because in the first place Linda struck me as perfectly innocent, and because in the second I wasn't paid, in the French phrase, for supposing Louisa Pallant much concerned on that score. The last hypothesis I should have invoked was that of private despair at bad moral symptoms. And in relation to Linda's nature I had before me the daily spectacle of her manner with my nephew. It was as charming as it could be without betrayal of a desire to lead him on. She was as familiar as a cousin, but as a distant one--a cousin who had been brought up to observe degrees. She was so much cleverer than Archie that she couldn't help laughing at him, but she didn't laugh enough to exclude variety, being well aware,

no doubt, that a woman's cleverness most shines in contrast with a man's stupidity when she pretends to take that stupidity for her law. Linda Pallant moreover
was not a chatterbox; as she knew the value of many things she knew the value of
intervals. There were a good many in the conversation of these young persons; my
nephew's own speech, to say nothing of his thought, abounding in comfortable
lapses; so that I sometimes wondered how their association was kept at that pitch of
continuity of which it gave the impression. It was friendly enough, evidently, when
Archie sat near her--near enough for low murmurs, had such risen to his lips--and
watched her with interested eyes and with freedom not to try too hard to make
himself agreeable. She had always something in hand--a flower in her tapestry to
finish, the leaves of a magazine to cut, a button to sew on her glove (she carried a
little work-bag in her pocket and was a person of the daintiest habits), a pencil to
ply ever so neatly in a sketchbook which she rested on her knee. When we were
indoors--mainly then at her mother's modest rooms--she had always the resource
of her piano, of which she was of course a perfect mistress.

These pursuits supported her, they helped her to an assurance under such nar-
row inspection--I ended by rebuking Archie for it; I told him he stared the poor
girl out of countenance--and she sought further relief in smiling all over the place.
When my young man's eyes shone at her those of Miss Pallant addressed themselves brightly to the trees and clouds and other surrounding objects, including her
mother and me. Sometimes she broke into a sudden embarrassed happy pointless
laugh. When she wandered off with him she looked back at us in a manner that
promised it wasn't for long and that she was with us still in spirit. If I liked her I
had therefore my good reason: it was many a day since a pretty girl had had the air
of taking me so much into account. Sometimes when they were so far away as not
to disturb us she read aloud a little to Mr. Archie. I don't know where she got her
books--I never provided them, and certainly he didn't. He was no reader and I fear
he often dozed.

III

I remember the first time--it was at the end of about ten days of this--that Mrs. Pallant remarked to me: "My dear friend, you're quite AMAZING! You behave for all the world as if you were perfectly ready to accept certain consequences." She nodded in the direction of our young companions, but I nevertheless put her at the pains of saying what consequences she meant. "What consequences? Why the very same consequences that ensued when you and I first became acquainted."

I hesitated, but then, looking her in the eyes, said: "Do you mean she'd throw him over?"

"You're not kind, you're not generous," she replied with a quick colour. "I'm giving you a warning."

"You mean that my boy may fall in love with your girl?"

"Certainly. It looks even as if the harm might be already done."

"Then your warning comes too late," I significantly smiled. "But why do you call it a harm?"

"Haven't you any sense of the rigour of your office?" she asked. "Is that what his mother has sent him out to you for: that you shall find him the first wife you can pick up, that you shall let him put his head into the noose the day after his arrival?"

"Heaven forbid I should do anything of the kind! I know moreover that his mother doesn't want him to marry young. She holds it the worst of mistakes, she feels that at that age a man never really chooses. He doesn't choose till he has lived a while, till he has looked about and compared."

"And what do you think then yourself?"

"I should like to say I regard the fact of falling in love, at whatever age, as in itself an act of selection. But my being as I am at this time of day would contradict me too much."

"Well then, you're too primitive. You ought to leave this place tomorrow."

"So as not to see Archie fall--?"

"You ought to fish him out now--from where he HAS fallen--and take him straight away."

I wondered a little. "Do you think he's in very far?"

"If I were his mother I know what I should think. I can put myself in her place--I'm not narrow-minded. I know perfectly well how she must regard such a question."

"And don't you know," I returned, "that in America that's not thought important--the way the mother regards it?"

Mrs. Pallant had a pause--as if I mystified or vexed her. "Well, we're not in America. We happen to be here."

"No; my poor sister's up to her neck in New York."

"I'm almost capable of writing to her to come out," said Mrs. Pallant.

"You ARE warning me," I cried, "but I hardly know of what! It seems to me my responsibility would begin only at the moment your daughter herself should seem in danger."

"Oh you needn't mind that--I'll take care of Linda."

But I went on. "If you think she's in danger already I'll carry him off to-morrow."

"It would be the best thing you could do."

"I don't know--I should be very sorry to act on a false alarm. I'm very well here; I like the place and the life and your society. Besides, it doesn't strike me that--on her side--there's any real symptom."

She looked at me with an air I had never seen in her face, and if I had puzzled her she repaid me in kind. "You're very annoying. You don't deserve what I'd fain do for you."

What she'd fain do for me she didn't tell me that day, but we took up the subject again. I remarked that I failed to see why we should assume that a girl like Linda--brilliant enough to make one of the greatest--would fall so very easily into my nephew's arms. Might I enquire if her mother had won a confession from her, if she had stammered out her secret? Mrs. Pallant made me, on this, the point that they had no need to tell each other such things--they hadn't lived together twenty years in such intimacy for nothing. To which I returned that I had guessed as much, but that there might be an exception for a great occasion like the present. If Linda had shown nothing it was a sign that for HER the occasion wasn't great; and I mentioned that Archie had spoken to me of the young lady only to remark casually and rather patronisingly, after his first encounter with her, that she was a regular little flower. (The little flower was nearly three years older than himself.) Apart from this he hadn't alluded to her and had taken up no allusion of mine. Mrs. Pallant informed me again--for which I was prepared--that I was quite too primitive; after which she said: "We needn't discuss the case if you don't wish to, but I happen to know--how I obtained my knowledge isn't important--that the moment Mr. Parker should propose to my daughter she'd gobble him down. Surely it's a detail worth mentioning to you."

I sought to defer then to her judgement. "Very good. I'll sound him. I'll look into the matter tonight."

"Don't, don't; you'll spoil everything!" She spoke as with some finer view. "Remove him quickly--that's the only thing."

I didn't at all like the idea of removing him quickly; it seemed too summary, too extravagant, even if presented to him on specious grounds; and moreover, as I had told Mrs. Pallant, I really had no wish to change my scene. It was no part of my promise to my sister that, with my middle-aged habits, I should duck and dodge about Europe. So I temporised. "Should you really object to the boy so much as a son-in-law? After all he's a good fellow and a gentleman."

"My poor friend, you're incredibly superficial!" she made answer with an assurance that struck me.

The contempt in it so nettled me in fact that I exclaimed: "Possibly! But it seems odd that a lesson in consistency should come from YOU."

I had no retort from her on this, rather to my surprise, and when she spoke again it was all quietly. "I think Linda and I had best withdraw. We've been here a month--it will have served our purpose."

"Mercy on us, that will be a bore!" I protested; and for the rest of the evening, till we separated--our conversation had taken place after dinner at the Kursaal--she

said little, preserving a subdued and almost injured air. This somehow didn't appeal
to me, since it was absurd that Louisa Pallant, of all women, should propose to put
me in the wrong. If ever a woman had been in the wrong herself--! I had even no
need to go into that. Archie and I, at all events, usually attended the ladies back to
their own door--they lived in a street of minor accommodation at a certain distance
from the Rooms--where we parted for the night late, on the big cobblestones, in
the little sleeping German town, under the closed windows of which, suggesting
stuffy interiors, our cheerful English partings resounded. On this occasion indeed
they rather languished; the question that had come up for me with Mrs. Pallant
appeared--and by no intention of mine--to have brushed the young couple with its
chill. Archie and Linda too struck me as conscious and dumb.

As I walked back to our hotel with my nephew I passed my hand into his arm
and put to him, by no roundabout approach, the question of whether he were in
serious peril of love.

"I don't know, I don't know--really, uncle, I don't know!" was, however, all
the satisfaction I could extract from the youth, who hadn't the smallest vein of
introspection. He mightn't know, but before we reached the inn--we had a few
more words on the subject--it seemed to me that *I* did. His mind wasn't formed
to accommodate at one time many subjects of thought, but Linda Pallant certainly
constituted for the moment its principal furniture. She pervaded his consciousness,
she solicited his curiosity, she associated herself, in a manner as yet informal and
undefined, with his future. I could see that she held, that she beguiled him as no
one had ever done. I didn't betray to him, however, that perception, and I spent my
night a prey to the consciousness that, after all, it had been none of my business to
provide him with the sense of being captivated. To put him in relation with a young
enchantress was the last thing his mother had expected of me or that I had expected
of myself. Moreover it was quite my opinion that he himself was too young to be
a judge of enchantresses. Mrs. Pallant was right and I had given high proof of lev-
ity in regarding her, with her beautiful daughter, as a "resource." There were other
resources--one of which WOULD be most decidedly to clear out. What did I know
after all about the girl except that I rejoiced to have escaped from marrying her
mother? That mother, it was true, was a singular person, and it was strange her
conscience should have begun to fidget in advance of my own. It was strange she

should so soon have felt Archie's peril, and even stranger that she should have then wished to "save" him. The ways of women were infinitely subtle, and it was no novelty to me that one never knew where they would turn up. As I haven't hesitated in this report to expose the irritable side of my own nature I shall confess that I even wondered if my old friend's solicitude hadn't been a deeper artifice. Wasn't it possibly a plan of her own for making sure of my young man--though I didn't quite see the logic of it? If she regarded him, which she might in view of his large fortune, as a great catch, mightn't she have arranged this little comedy, in their personal interest, with the girl?

That possibility at any rate only made it a happier thought that I should win my companion to some curiosity about other places. There were many of course much more worth his attention than Homburg. In the course of the morning--it was after our early luncheon--I walked round to Mrs. Pallant's to let her know I was ready to take action; but even while I went I again felt the unlikelihood of the part attributed by my fears and by the mother's own, so far as they had been roused, to Linda. Certainly if she was such a girl as these fears represented her she would fly at higher game. It was with an eye to high game, Mrs. Pallant had frankly admitted to me, that she had been trained, and such an education, to say nothing of such a performer, justified a hope of greater returns. A young American, the fruit of scant "modelling," who could give her nothing but pocket-money, was a very moderate prize, and if she had been prepared to marry for ambition--there was no such hardness in her face or tone, but then there never is--her mark would be inevitably a "personage" quelconque. I was received at my friend's lodging with the announcement that she had left Homburg with her daughter half an hour before. The good woman who had entertained the pair professed to know nothing of their movements beyond the fact that they had gone to Frankfort, where, however, it was her belief that they didn't intend to remain. They were evidently travelling beyond. Sudden, their decision to move? Oh yes, the matter of a moment. They must have spent the night in packing, they had so many things and such pretty ones; and their poor maid, all the morning, had scarce had time to swallow her coffee. But they clearly were ladies accustomed to come and go. It didn't matter--with such rooms as hers she never wanted: there was a new family coming in at three.

IV

This piece of strategy left me staring and made me, I must confess, quite furious. My only consolation was that Archie, when I told him, looked as blank as myself, and that the trick touched him more nearly, for I was not now in love with Louisa. We agreed that we required an explanation and we pretended to expect one the next day in the shape of a letter satisfactory even to the point of being apologetic. When I say "we" pretended I mean that I did, for my suspicion that he knew what had been on foot--through an arrangement with Linda--lasted only a moment. If his resentment was less than my own his surprise was equally great. I had been willing to bolt, but I felt slighted by the ease with which Mrs. Pallant had shown she could part with us. Archie professed no sense of a grievance, because in the first place he was shy about it and because in the second it was evidently not definite to him that he had been encouraged--equipped as he was, I think, with no very particular idea of what constituted encouragement. He was fresh from the wonderful country in which there may between the ingenuous young be so little question of "intentions." He was but dimly conscious of his own and could by no means have told me whether he had been challenged or been jilted. I didn't want to exasperate him, but when at the end of three days more we were still without news of our late companions I observed that it was very simple:--they must have been just hiding from us; they thought us dangerous; they wished to avoid entanglements. They had found us too attentive and wished not to raise false hopes. He appeared to accept this explanation and even had the air--so at least I inferred from his asking me no questions--of judging the matter might be delicate for myself. The poor youth was altogether much mystified, and I smiled at the image in his mind of Mrs. Pallant fleeing from his uncle's importunities. We decided to leave Homburg, but if we didn't pursue our fugitives it wasn't simply that we were ignorant of where they were. I could have found that out with a little trouble, but I was deterred by the reflexion that this would be Louisa's reasoning. She was a dreadful humbug and her departure had been a provocation--I fear it was in that stupid conviction that I made out a little independent itinerary with Archie. I even believed we should learn where they were quite soon enough, and that our patience--even my young man's--would be longer than theirs. Therefore I uttered a small private cry of triumph when three weeks later--we happened to be at Interlaken--he reported to me that he had received a note from Miss Pallant. The form of this confidence was his enquiring if there were particular reasons why we should longer delay our projected visit to the Italian lakes. Mightn't the fear of the hot weather, which was moreover at that season our native temperature, cease to operate, the middle of September having arrived? I answered that we would start on the morrow if he liked, and then, pleased apparently that I was so easy to deal with, he revealed his little secret. He showed me his letter, which was a graceful natural document--it covered with a few flowing strokes but a single page of note-paper--not at all compromising to the young lady. If, however, it was almost the apology I had looked for--save that this should have come from the mother--it was not ostensibly in the least an invitation. It mentioned casually--the mention was mainly in the words at the head of her paper--that they were on the Lago Maggiore, at Baveno; but it consisted mainly of the expression of a regret that they had had so abruptly to leave Homburg. Linda failed to say under what necessity they had found themselves; she only hoped we hadn't judged them too harshly and would accept "this hasty line" as a substitute for the omitted good-bye. She also hoped our days were passing pleasantly and with the same lovely weather that prevailed south of the Alps; and she remained very sincerely and with the kindest remembrances--!

The note contained no message from her mother, and it was open to me to suppose, as I should prefer, either that Mrs. Pallant hadn't known she was writing or that they wished to make us think she hadn't known. The letter might pass as a common civility of the girl's to a person with whom she had been on easy terms. It was, however, for something more than this that my nephew took it; so at least I gathered from the touching candour of his determination to go to Baveno. I judged it idle to drag him another way; he had money in his own pocket and was quite capable of giving me the slip. Yet--such are the sweet incongruities of youth--when

I asked him to what tune he had been thinking of Linda since they left us in the lurch he replied: "Oh I haven't been thinking at all! Why should I?" This fib was accompanied by an exorbitant blush. Since he was to obey his young woman's signal I must equally make out where it would take him, and one splendid morning we started over the Simplon in a post-chaise.

I represented to him successfully that it would be in much better taste for us to alight at Stresa, which as every one knows is a resort of tourists, also on the shore of the major lake, at about a mile's distance from Baveno. If we stayed at the latter place we should have to inhabit the same hotel as our friends, and this might be awkward in view of a strained relation with them. Nothing would be easier than to go and come between the two points, especially by the water, which would give Archie a chance for unlimited paddling. His face lighted up at the vision of a pair of oars; he pretended to take my plea for discretion very seriously, and I could see that he had at once begun to calculate opportunities for navigation with Linda. Our post-chaise--I had insisted on easy stages and we were three days on the way--deposited us at Stresa toward the middle of the afternoon, and it was within an amazingly short time that I found myself in a small boat with my nephew, who pulled us over to Baveno with vigorous strokes. I remember the sweetness of the whole impression. I had had it before, but to my companion it was new, and he thought it as pretty as the opera: the enchanting beauty of the place and, hour, the stillness of the air and water, with the romantic fantastic Borromean Islands set as great jewels in a crystal globe. We disembarked at the steps by the garden-foot of the hotel, and somehow it seemed a perfectly natural part of the lovely situation that I should immediately become conscious of Mrs. Pallant and her daughter seated on the terrace and quietly watching us. They had the air of expectation, which I think we had counted on. I hadn't even asked Archie if he had answered Linda's note; this was between themselves and in the way of supervision I had done enough in coming with him.

There is no doubt our present address, all round, lacked a little the easiest grace--or at least Louisa's and mine did. I felt too much the appeal of her exhibition to notice closely the style of encounter of the young people. I couldn't get it out of my head, as I have sufficiently indicated, that Mrs. Pallant was playing a game, and I'm afraid she saw in my face that this suspicion had been the motive of my journey. I had come there to find her out. The knowledge of my purpose couldn't help her to make me very welcome, and that's why I speak of our meeting constrainedly. We observed none the less all the forms, and the admirable scene left us plenty to talk about. I made no reference before Linda to the retreat from Homburg. This young woman looked even prettier than she had done on the eve of that manoeuvre and gave no sign of an awkward consciousness. She again so struck me as a charming clever girl that I was freshly puzzled to know why we should get--or should have got--into a tangle about her. People had to want to complicate a situation to do it on so simple a pretext as that Linda was in every way beautiful. This was the clear fact: so why shouldn't the presumptions be in favour of every result of it? One of the effects of that cause, on the spot, was that at the end of a very short time Archie proposed to her to take a turn with him in his boat, which awaited us at the foot of the steps. She looked at her mother with a smiling "May I, mamma?" and Mrs. Pallant answered "Certainly, darling, if you're not afraid." At this--I scarcely knew why--I sought the relief of laughter: it must have affected me as comic that the girl's general competence should suffer the imputation of that particular flaw. She gave me a quick slightly sharp look as she turned away with my nephew; it appeared to challenge me a little--"Pray what's the matter with YOU?" It was the first expression of the kind I had ever seen in her face. Mrs. Pallant's attention, on the other hand, rather strayed from me; after we had been left there together she sat silent, not heeding me, looking at the lake and mountains--at the snowy crests crowned with the flush of evening. She seemed not even to follow our young companions as they got into their boat and pushed off. For some minutes I respected her mood; I walked slowly up and down the terrace and lighted a cigar, as she had always permitted me to do at Homburg. I found in her, it was true, rather a new air of weariness; her fine cold well-bred face was pale; I noted in it new lines of fatigue, almost of age. At last I stopped in front of her and--since she looked so sad--asked if she had been having bad news.

"The only bad news was when I learned--through your nephew's note to Linda--that you were coming to us."

"Ah then he wrote?"

"Certainly he wrote."

"You take it all harder than I do," I returned as I sat down beside her. And then

I added, smiling: "Have you written to his mother?"

Slowly at last, and more directly, she faced me. "Take care, take care, or you'll have been more brutal than you'll afterwards like," she said with an air of patience before the inevitable.

"Never, never! Unless you think me brutal if I ask whether you knew when Linda wrote."

She had an hesitation. "Yes, she showed me her letter. She wouldn't have done anything else. I let it go because I didn't know what course was best. I'm afraid to oppose her to her face."

"Afraid, my dear friend, with that girl?"

"That girl? Much you know about her! It didn't follow you'd come. I didn't take that for granted."

"I'm like you," I said--"I too am afraid of my nephew. I don't venture to oppose him to his face. The only thing I could do--once he wished it--was to come with him."

"I see. Well, there are grounds, after all, on which I'm glad," she rather inscrutably added.

"Oh I was conscientious about that! But I've no authority; I can neither drive him nor stay him--I can use no force," I explained. "Look at the way he's pulling that boat and see if you can fancy me."

"You could tell him she's a bad hard girl--one who'd poison any good man's life!" my companion broke out with a passion that startled me.

At first I could only gape. "Dear lady, what do you mean?"

She bent her face into her hands, covering it over with them, and so remained a minute; then she continued a little differently, though as if she hadn't heard my question: "I hoped you were too disgusted with us--after the way we left you planted."

"It was disconcerting assuredly, and it might have served if Linda hadn't written. That patched it up," I gaily professed. But my gaiety was thin, for I was still amazed at her violence of a moment before. "Do you really mean that she won't do?" I added.

She made no direct answer; she only said after a little that it didn't matter whether the crisis should come a few weeks sooner or a few weeks later, since it was destined to come at the first chance, the favouring moment. Linda had marked my young man--and when Linda had marked a thing!

"Bless my soul--how very grim--" But I didn't understand. "Do you mean she's in love with him?"

"It's enough if she makes him think so--though even that isn't essential."

Still I was at sea. "If she makes him think so? Dear old friend, what's your idea? I've observed her, I've watched her, and when all's said what has she done? She has been civil and pleasant to him, but it would have been much more marked if she hadn't. She has really shown him, with her youth and her natural charm, nothing more than common friendliness. Her note was nothing; he let me see it."

"I don't think you've heard every word she has said to him," Mrs. Pallant returned with an emphasis that still struck me as perverse.

"No more have you, I take it!" I promptly cried. She evidently meant more than she said; but if this excited my curiosity it also moved, in a different connexion, my indulgence.

"No, but I know my own daughter. She's a most remarkable young woman."

"You've an extraordinary tone about her," I declared "such a tone as I think I've never before heard on a mother's lips. I've had the same impression from you--that of a disposition to 'give her away,' but never yet so strong."

At this Mrs. Pallant got up; she stood there looking down at me. "You make my reparation--my expiation--difficult!" And leaving me still more astonished she moved along the terrace.

I overtook her presently and repeated her words. "Your reparation--your expiation? What on earth are you talking about?"

"You know perfectly what I mean--it's too magnanimous of you to pretend you don't."

"Well, at any rate," I said, "I don't see what good it does me, or what it makes up to me for, that you should abuse your daughter."

"Oh I don't care; I shall save him!" she cried as we went, and with an extravagance, as I felt, of sincerity. At the same moment two ladies, apparently English, came toward us--scattered groups had been sitting there and the inmates of the hotel were moving to and fro--and I observed the immediate charming transition, the fruit of such years of social practice, by which, as they greeted us, her tension and her impatience dropped to recognition and pleasure. They stopped to speak to her and she enquired with sweet propriety as to the "continued improvement" of their sister. I strolled on and she presently rejoined me; after which she had a peremptory note. "Come away from this--come down into the garden." We descended to that blander scene, strolled through it and paused on the border of the lake.

V

The charm of the evening had deepened, the stillness was like a solemn expression on a beautiful face and the whole air of the place divine. In the fading light my nephew's boat was too far out to be perceived. I looked for it a little and then, as I gave it up, remarked that from such an excursion as that, on such a lake and at such an hour, a young man and a young woman of common sensibility could only come back doubly pledged to each other.

To this observation Mrs. Pallant's answer was, superficially at least, irrelevant; she said after a pause: "With you, my dear man, one has certainly to dot one's 'i's.' Haven't you discovered, and didn't I tell you at Homburg, that we're miserably poor?"

"Isn't 'miserably' rather too much--living as you are at an expensive hotel?"

Well, she promptly met this. "They take us en pension, for ever so little a day. I've been knocking about Europe long enough to learn all sorts of horrid arts. Besides, don't speak of hotels; we've spent half our life in them and Linda told me only last night that she hoped never to put her foot into one again. She feels that when she comes to such a place as this she ought, if things were decently right, to find a villa of her own."

"Then her companion there's perfectly competent to give her one. Don't think I've the least desire to push them into each other's arms--I only ask to wash my hands of them. But I should like to know why you want, as you said just now, to save him. When you speak as if your daughter were a monster I take it you're not serious."

She was facing me in the rich short twilight, and to describe herself as immeasurably more serious perhaps than she had ever been in her life she had only to look at me without protestation. "It's Linda's standard. God knows I myself could get on! She's ambitious, luxurious, determined to have what she wants--more 'on the make' than any one I've ever seen. Of course it's open to you to tell me it's my own fault, that I was so before her and have made her so. But does that make me like it any better?"

"Dear Mrs. Pallant, you're wonderful, you're terrible," I could only stammer, lost in the desert of my thoughts.

"Oh yes, you've made up your mind about me; you see me in a certain way and don't like the trouble of changing. Votre siege est fait. But you'll HAVE to change--if you've any generosity!" Her eyes shone in the summer dusk and the beauty of her youth came back to her.

"Is this a part of the reparation, of the expiation?" I demanded. "I don't see what you ever did to Archie."

"It's enough that he belongs to you. But it isn't for you I do it--it's for myself," she strangely went on.

"Doubtless you've your own reasons--which I can't penetrate. But can't you sacrifice something else? Must you sacrifice your only child?"

"My only child's my punishment, my only child's my stigma!" she cried in her exaltation.

"It seems to me rather that you're hers."

"Hers? What does SHE know of such things?--what can she ever feel? She's cased in steel; she has a heart of marble. It's true--it's true," said Louisa Pallant. "She appals me!"

I laid my hand on my poor friend's; I uttered, with the intention of checking and soothing her, the first incoherent words that came into my head and I drew her toward a bench a few steps away. She dropped upon it; I placed myself near her and besought her to consider well what she said. She owed me nothing and I wished no one injured, no one denounced or exposed for my sake.

"For your sake? Oh I'm not thinking of you!" she answered; and indeed the next moment I thought my words rather fatuous. "It's a satisfaction to my own con- science--for I HAVE one, little as you may think I've a right to speak of it. I've been punished by my sin itself. I've been hideously worldly, I've thought only of that, and I've taught her to be so--to do the same. That's the only instruction I've ever given her, and she has learned the lesson so well that now I see it stamped there in all her nature, on all her spirit and on all her form, I'm horrified at my work. For years we've lived that way; we've thought of nothing else. She has profited so well by my beautiful influence that she has gone far beyond the great original. I say I'm horrified," Mrs. Pallant dreadfully wound up, "because she's horrible."

"My poor extravagant friend," I pleaded, "isn't it still more so to hear a mother say such things?"

"Why so, if they're abominably true? Besides, I don't care what I say if I save him."

I could only gape again at this least expected of all my adventures. "Do you expect me then to repeat to him--?"

"Not in the least," she broke in; "I'll do it myself." At this I uttered some strong inarticulate protest, but she went on with the grimmest simplicity: "I was very glad at first, but it would have been better if we hadn't met."

"I don't agree to that, for you interest me," I rather ruefully professed, "immensely."

"I don't care if I do--so I interest HIM."

"You must reflect then that your denunciation can only strike me as, for all its violence, vague and unconvincing. Never had a girl less the appearance of bearing such charges out. You know how I've admired her."

"You know nothing about her! *I* do, you see, for she's the work of my hand!" And Mrs. Pallant laughed for bitterness. "I've watched her for years, and little by little, for the last two or three, it has come over me. There's not a tender spot in her whole composition. To arrive at a brilliant social position, if it were necessary, she would see me drown in this lake without lifting a finger, she would stand there and see it--she would push me in--and never feel a pang. That's my young lady!" Her lucidity chilled me to the soul--it seemed to shine so flawless. "To climb up to the top and be splendid and envied there," she went on--"to do that at any cost or by any meanness and cruelty is the only thing she has a heart for. She'd lie for it, she'd steal for it, she'd kill for it!" My companion brought out these words with a cold confidence that had evidently behind it some occult past process of growth. I watched her pale face and glowing eyes; she held me breathless and frowning, but her strange vindictive, or at least retributive, passion irresistibly imposed itself. I found myself at last believing her, pitying her more than I pitied the subject of her dreadful analysis. It was as if she had held her tongue for longer than she could bear, suffering more and more the importunity of the truth. It relieved her thus to drag that to the light, and still she kept up the high and most unholy sacrifice. "God in his mercy has let me see it in time, but his ways are strange that he has let me see it in my daughter. It's myself he has let me see--myself as I was for years. But she's worse--she IS, I assure you; she's worse than I intended or dreamed." Her hands were clasped tightly together in her lap; her low voice quavered and her breath came short; she looked up at the southern stars as if THEY would understand.

"Have you ever spoken to her as you speak to me?" I finally asked. "Have you ever put before her this terrible arraignment?"

"Put it before her? How can I put it before her when all she would have to say would be: 'You, YOU, you base one, who made me--?'"

"Then why do you want to play her a trick?"

"I'm not bound to tell you, and you wouldn't see my point if I did. I should play that boy a far worse one if I were to stay my hand."

Oh I had my view of this. "If he loves her he won't believe a word you say."

"Very possibly, but I shall have done my duty."

"And shall you say to him," I asked, "simply what you've said to me?"

"Never mind what I shall say to him. It will be something that will perhaps helpfully affect him. Only," she added with her proud decision, "I must lose no time."

"If you're so bent on gaining time," I said, "why did you let her go out in the boat with him?"

"Let her? how could I prevent it?"

"But she asked your permission."

"Ah that," she cried, "is all a part of all the comedy!"

It fairly hushed me to silence, and for a moment more she said nothing. "Then she doesn't know you hate her?" I resumed.

"I don't know what she knows. She has depths and depths, and all of them bad. Besides, I don't hate her in the least; I just pity her for what I've made of her. But I pity still more the man who may find himself married to her."

"There's not much danger of there being any such person," I wailed, "at the rate you go on."

"I beg your pardon--there's a perfect possibility," said my companion. "She'll marry--she'll marry 'well.' She'll marry a title as well as a fortune.

"It's a pity my nephew hasn't a title," I attempted the grimace of suggesting.

She seemed to wonder. "I see you think I want that, and that I'm acting a part. God forgive you! Your suspicion's perfectly natural. How can any one TELL," asked Louisa Pallant--"with people like us?"

Her utterance of these words brought tears to my eyes. I laid my hand on her arm, holding her a while, and we looked at each other through the dusk. "You couldn't do more if he were my son."

"Oh if he had been your son he'd have kept out of it! I like him for himself. He's simple and sane and honest--he needs affection."

"He would have quite the most remarkable of mothers-in-law!" I commented.

Mrs. Pallant gave a small dry laugh--she wasn't joking. We lingered by the lake while I thought over what she had said to me and while she herself apparently thought. I confess that even close at her side and under the strong impression of her sincerity, her indifference to the conventional graces, my imagination, my constitutional scepticism began to range. Queer ideas came into my head. Was the comedy on HER side and not on the girl's, and was she posturing as a magnanimous woman at poor Linda's expense? Was she determined, in spite of the young lady's preference, to keep her daughter for a grander personage than a young American whose dollars were not numerous enough--numerous as they were--to make up for his want of high relationships, and had she invented at once the boldest and the subtlest of games in order to keep the case in her hands? If she was prepared really to address herself to Archie she would have to go very far to overcome the mistrust he would be sure to feel at a proceeding superficially so sinister? Was she prepared to go far enough? The answer to these doubts was simply the way I had been touched--it came back to me the next moment--when she used the words "people like us." Their effect was to wring my heart. She seemed to kneel in the dust, and I felt in a manner ashamed that I had let her sink to it. She said to me at last that I must wait no longer, I must go away before the young people came back. They were staying long, too long; all the more reason then she should deal with my nephew that night. I must drive back to Stresa, or if I liked I could go on foot: it wasn't far--for an active man. She disposed of me freely, she was so full of her purpose; and after we had quitted the garden and returned to the terrace above she seemed almost to push me to leave her--I felt her fine consecrated hands fairly quiver on my shoulders. I was ready to do as she prescribed; she affected me painfully, she had given me a "turn," and I wanted to get away from her. But before I went I asked her why Linda should regard my young man as such a parti; it didn't square after all with her account of the girl's fierce ambitions. By that account these favours to one so graceless were a woeful waste of time.

"Oh she has worked it all out; she has regarded the question in every light," said Mrs. Pallant. "If she has made up her mind it's because she sees what she can do."

"Do you mean that she has talked it over with you?"

My friend's wonderful face pitied my simplicity. "Lord! for what do you take us? We don't talk things over to-day. We know each other's point of view and only have to act. We observe the highest proprieties of speech. We never for a moment name anything ugly--we only just go at it. We can take definitions, which are awkward things, for granted."

"But in this case," I nevertheless urged, "the poor thing can't possibly be aware of your point of view."

"No," she conceded--"that's because I haven't played fair. Of course she couldn't expect I'd cheat. There ought to be honour among thieves. But it was open to her to do the same."

"What do you mean by the same?"

"She might have fallen in love with a poor man. Then I should have been 'done.'"

"A rich one's better; he can do more," I replied with conviction.

At this she appeared to have, in the oddest way, a momentary revulsion. "So you'd have reason to know if you had led the life that we have! Never to have had really enough--I mean to do just the few simple things we've wanted; never to have had the sinews of war, I suppose you'd call them, the funds for a campaign; to have felt every day and every hour the hard eternal pinch and found the question of dollars and cents--and so horridly few of them--mixed up with every experience, with every impulse: that DOES make one mercenary, does make money seem a good beyond all others; which it's quite natural it should! And it's why Linda's of the opinion that a fortune's always a fortune. She knows all about that of your nephew, how it's invested, how it may be expected to increase, exactly on what sort of footing it would enable her to live. She has decided that it's enough, and enough is as good as a feast. She thinks she could lead him by the nose, and I dare say she could. She'll of course make him live in these countries; she hasn't the slightest intention of casting her pearls--but basta!" said my friend. "I think she has views upon London, because in England he can hunt and shoot, and that will make him leave her more or less to herself."

"I don't know about his leaving her to herself, but it strikes me that he would like the rest of that matter very much," I returned. "That's not at all a bad programme even from Archie's point of view."

"It's no use thinking of princes," she pursued as if she hadn't heard me. "They're most of them more in want of money even than we. Therefore 'greatness' is out of the question--we really recognised that at an early stage. Your nephew's exactly the sort of young man we've always built upon--if he wasn't, so impossibly, your nephew. From head to foot he was made on purpose. Dear Linda was her mother's own daughter when she recognised him on the spot! One's enough of a prince to-day when one's the right American: such a wonderful price is set on one's not being the wrong! It does as well as anything and it's a great simplification. If you don't believe me go to London and see." She had come with me out to the road. I had said I would walk back to Stresa and we stood there in the sweet dark warmth. As I took her hand, bidding her good-night, I couldn't but exhale a compassion. "Poor Linda, poor Linda!"

"Oh she'll live to do better," said Mrs. Pallant.

"How can she do better--since you've described all she finds Archie as perfection?"

She knew quite what she meant. "Ah better for HIM!"

I still had her hand--I still sought her eyes. "How came it you could throw me over--such a woman as you?"

"Well, my friend, if I hadn't thrown you over how could I do this for you?" On which, disengaging herself, she turned quickly away.

VI

I don't know how deeply she flushed as she made, in the form of her question, this avowal, which was a retraction of a former denial and the real truth, as I permitted myself to believe; but was aware of the colour of my own cheeks while I took my way to Stresa--a walk of half an hour--in the attenuating night. The new and singular character in which she had appeared to me produced in me an emotion that would have made sitting still in a carriage impossible. This same stress kept me up after I had reached my hotel; as I knew I shouldn't sleep it was useless to go to bed. Long, however, as I deferred this ceremony, Archie had not re-appeared when the inn-lights began here and there to be dispensed with. I felt even slightly anxious for him, wondering at possible mischances. Then I reflected that in case of an accident on the lake, that is of his continued absence from Baveno--Mrs. Pallant would already have dispatched me a messenger. It was foolish moreover to suppose anything could have happened to him after putting off from Baveno by water to rejoin me, for the evening was absolutely windless and more than suffi-ciently clear and the lake as calm as glass. Besides I had unlimited confidence in his power to take care of himself in a much tighter place. I went to my room at last; his own was at some distance, the people of the hotel not having been able--it was the height of the autumn season--to make us contiguous. Before I went to bed I had oc-casion to ring for a servant, and I then learned by a chance enquiry that my nephew had returned an hour before and had gone straight to his own quarters. I hadn't sup-posed he could come in without my seeing him--I was wandering about the saloons and terraces--and it had not occurred to me to knock at his door. I had half a mind to do so now--I was so anxious as to how I should find him; but I checked myself, for evidently he had wanted to dodge me. This didn't diminish my curiosity, and I slept even less than I had expected. His so markedly shirking our encounter--for if he hadn't perceived me downstairs he might have looked for me in my room--was a sign that Mrs. Pallant's interview with him would really have come off. What had she said to him? What strong measures had she taken? That almost morbid resolution I still seemed to hear the ring of pointed to conceivable extremities that I shrank from considering. She had spoken of these things while we parted there as something she would do for me; but I had made the mental comment in walking away from her that she hadn't done it yet. It wouldn't truly be done till Archie had truly backed out. Perhaps it was done by this time; his avoiding me seemed almost a proof. That was what I thought of most of the night. I spent a considerable part of it at my window, looking out to the couchant Alps. HAD he thought better of it?--was he making up his mind to think better of it? There was a strange contradiction in the matter; there were in fact more contradictions than ever. I had taken from Louisa what she told me of Linda, and yet that other idea made me ashamed of my nephew. I was sorry for the girl; I regretted her loss of a great chance, if loss it was to be; and yet I hoped her mother's grand treachery--I didn't know what to call it--had been at least, to her lover, thoroughgoing. It would need strong action in that lady to justify his retreat. For him too I was sorry--if she had made on him the impression she desired. Once or twice I was on the point of getting into my dressing-gown and going forth to condole with him. I was sure he too had jumped up from his bed and was looking out of his window at the everlasting hills.

But I am bound to say that when we met in the morning for breakfast he showed few traces of ravage. Youth is strange; it has resources that later experience seems only to undermine. One of these is the masterly resource of beautiful blankness. As we grow older and cleverer we think that too simple, too crude; we dissimulate more elaborately, but with an effect much less baffling. My young man looked not in the least as if he had lain awake or had something on his mind; and when I asked him what he had done after my premature departure--I explained this by saying I had been tired of waiting for him; fagged with my journey I had wanted to go to bed--he replied: "Oh nothing in particular. I hung about the place; I like it better than this one. We had an awfully jolly time on the water. *I* wasn't in the least fagged." I didn't worry him with questions; it struck me as gross to try to probe his secret. The only indication he gave was on my saying after breakfast that I should go over again to see our friends and my appearing to take for granted he would be glad to come too. Then he let fall that he'd stop at Stresa--he had paid them such a tremendous visit; also that he had arrears of letters. There was a freshness in his scruples about the length of his visits, and I knew something about his correspondence, which consisted entirely of twenty pages every week from his mother. But he soothed my anxiety so little that it was really this yearning that carried me back to Baveno. This time I ordered a conveyance, and as I got into it he stood watching me from the porch of the hotel with his hands in his pockets. Then it was for the first time that I saw in the poor youth's face the expression of a person slightly dazed, slightly foolish even, to whom something disagreeable has happened. Our eyes met as I observed him, and I was on the point of saying "You had really better come with me" when he turned away. He went into the house as to escape my call. I said to myself that he had been indeed warned off, but that it wouldn't take much to bring him back.

The servant to whom I spoke at Baveno described my friends as in a summerhouse in the garden, to which he led the way. The place at large had an empty air; most of the inmates of the hotel were dispersed on the lake, on the hills, in picnics, excursions, visits to the Borromean Islands. My guide was so far right as that Linda was in the summer-house, but she was there alone. On finding this the case I stopped short, rather awkwardly--I might have been, from the way I suddenly felt, an unmasked hypocrite, a proved conspirator against her security and honour. But there was no embarrassment in lovely Linda; she looked up with a cry of pleasure from the book she was reading and held out her hand with engaging frankness. I felt again as if I had no right to that favour, which I pretended not to have noticed. This gave no chill, however, to her pretty manner; she moved a roll of tapestry off the bench so that I might sit down; she praised the place as a delightful shady corner. She had never been fresher, fairer, kinder; she made her mother's awful talk about her a hideous dream. She told me her mother was coming to join her; she had remained indoors to write a letter. One couldn't write out there, though it was so nice in other respects: the table refused to stand firm. They too then had pretexts of letters between them--I judged this a token that the situation was tense. It was the only one nevertheless that Linda gave: like Archie she was young enough to carry it off. She had been used to seeing us always together, yet she made no comment on my having come over without him. I waited in vain for her to speak of this--it would only be natural; her omission couldn't but have a sense. At last I remarked that my nephew was very unsociable that morning; I had expected him to join me, but he hadn't seemed to see the attraction.

"I'm very glad. You can tell him that if you like," said Linda Pallant.

I wondered at her. "If I tell him he'll come at once."

"Then don't tell him; I don't want him to come. He stayed too long last night," she went on, "and kept me out on the water till I don't know what o'clock. That sort of thing isn't done here, you know, and every one was shocked when we came back--or rather, you see, when we didn't! I begged him to bring me in, but he wouldn't. When we did return--I almost had to take the oars myself--I felt as if every one had been sitting up to time us, to stare at us. It was awfully awkward."

These words much impressed me; and as I have treated the reader to most of the reflexions--some of them perhaps rather morbid--in which I indulged on the subject of this young lady and her mother, I may as well complete the record and let him know that I now wondered whether Linda--candid and accomplished maiden--entertained the graceful thought of strengthening her hold of Archie by attempting to prove he had "compromised" her. "Ah no doubt that was the reason he had a bad conscience last evening!" I made answer. "When he came back to Stresa he sneaked off to his room; he wouldn't look me in the face."

But my young lady was not to be ruffled. "Mamma was so vexed that she took him apart and gave him a scolding. And to punish ME she sent me straight to bed. She has very old-fashioned ideas--haven't you, mamma?" she added, looking over my head at Mrs. Pallant, who had just come in behind me.

I forget how her mother met Linda's appeal; Louisa stood there with two letters, sealed and addressed, in her hand. She greeted me gaily and then asked her daughter if she were possessed of postage-stamps. Linda consulted a well-worn little pocket-book and confessed herself destitute; whereupon her mother gave her the letters with the request that she would go into the hotel, buy the proper stamps at the office, carefully affix them and put the letters into the box. She was to pay for the stamps, not have them put on the bill--a preference for which Mrs. Pallant gave reasons. I had bought some at Stresa that morning and was on the point of offering them when, apparently having guessed my intention, the elder lady silenced me with a look. Linda announced without reserve that she hadn't money and Louisa then fumbled for a franc. When she had found and bestowed it the girl kissed her before going off with the letters.

"Darling mother, you haven't any too many of them, have you?" she murmured; and she gave me, sidelong, as she left us, the prettiest half-comical, half-pitiful smile.

"She's amazing--she's amazing," said Mrs. Pallant as we looked at each other.

"Does she know what you've done?"

"She knows I've done something and she's making up her mind what it is. She'll satisfy herself in the course of the next twenty-four hours--if your nephew doesn't come back. I think I can promise you he won't."

"And won't she ask you?"

"Never!"

"Shan't you tell her? Can you sit down together in this summer-house, this divine day, with such a dreadful thing as that between you?"

My question found my friend quite ready. "Don't you remember what I told you about our relations--that everything was implied between us and nothing expressed? The ideas we have had in common--our perpetual worldliness, our always looking out for chances--are not the sort of thing that can be uttered conveniently between persons who like to keep up forms, as we both do: so that, always, if we've understood each other it has been enough. We shall understand each other now, as we've always done, and nothing will be changed. There has always been something between us that couldn't be talked about."

"Certainly, she's amazing--she's amazing," I repeated; "but so are you." And then I asked her what she had said to my boy.

She seemed surprised. "Hasn't he told you?"

"No, and he never will."

"I'm glad of that," she answered simply.

"But I'm not sure he won't come back. He didn't this morning, but he had already half a mind to."

"That's your imagination," my companion said with her fine authority. "If you knew what I told him you'd be sure."

"And you won't let me know?"

"Never, dear friend."

"And did he believe you?"

"Time will show--but I think so."

"And how did you make it plausible to him that you should take so unnatural a course?"

For a moment she said nothing, only looking at me. Then at last: "I told him the truth."

"The truth?"

"Take him away--take him away!" she broke out. "That's why I got rid of Linda, to tell you you mustn't stay--you must leave Stresa to-morrow. This time it's you who must do it. I can't fly from you again--it costs too much!" And she smiled strangely.

"Don't be afraid; don't be afraid. We'll break camp again to-morrow--ah me! But I want to go myself," I added. I took her hand in farewell, but spoke again while I held it. "The way you put it, about Linda, was very bad?"

"It was horrible."

I turned away--I felt indeed that I couldn't stay. She kept me from going to the hotel, as I might meet Linda coming back, which I was far from wishing to do, and showed me another way into the road. Then she turned round to meet her daughter and spend the rest of the morning there with her, spend it before the bright blue lake and the snowy crests of the Alps. When I reached Stresa again I found my young man had gone off to Milan--to see the cathedral, the servant said--leaving a message for me to the effect that, as he shouldn't be back for a day or two, though there were numerous trains, he had taken a few clothes. The next day I received telegram-notice that he had determined to go on to Venice and begged I would forward the rest of his luggage. "Please don't come after me," this missive added; "I want to be alone; I shall do no harm." That sounded pathetic to me, in the light of what I knew, and I was glad to leave him to his own devices. He proceeded to Venice and I re-crossed the Alps. For several weeks after this I expected to discover that he had rejoined Mrs. Pallant; but when we met that November in Paris I saw he had nothing to hide from me save indeed the secret of what our extraordinary friend had said to him. This he concealed from me then and has concealed ever since. He returned to America before Christmas--when I felt the crisis over. I've never again seen the wronger of my youth. About a year after our more recent adventure her daughter Linda married, in London, a young Englishman the heir to a large fortune, a fortune acquired by his father in some prosaic but flourishing industry. Mrs. Gimingham's admired photographs--such is Linda's present name--may be obtained from the principal stationers. I am convinced her mother was sincere. My nephew has not even yet changed his state, my sister at last thinks it high time. I put before her as soon as I next saw her the incidents here recorded, and--such is the inconsequence of women--nothing can exceed her reprobation of Louisa Pallant.

The Codes Of Hammurabi And Moses
W. W. Davies

QTY

The discovery of the Hammurabi Code is one of the greatest achievements of archaeology, and is of paramount interest, not only to the student of the Bible, but also to all those interested in ancient history...

Religion   **ISBN:** *1-59462-338-4*   **Pages:132**

MSRP $12.95

The Theory of Moral Sentiments
Adam Smith

QTY

This work from 1749. contains original theories of conscience amd moral judgment and it is the foundation for systemof morals.

Philosophy **ISBN:** *1-59462-777-0*   **Pages:536**

MSRP $19.95

Jessica's First Prayer
Hesba Stretton

QTY

In a screened and secluded corner of one of the many railway-bridges which span the streets of London there could be seen a few years ago, from five o'clock every morning until half past eight, a tidily set-out coffee-stall, consisting of a trestle and board, upon which stood two large tin cans, with a small fire of charcoal burning under each so as to keep the coffee boiling during the early hours of the morning when the work-people were thronging into the city on their way to their daily toil...

Pages:84

Childrens   **ISBN:** *1-59462-373-2*   *MSRP $9.95*

My Life and Work
Henry Ford

QTY

Henry Ford revolutionized the world with his implementation of mass production for the Model T automobile. Gain valuable business insight into his life and work with his own auto-biography... "We have only started on our development of our country we have not as yet, with all our talk of wonderful progress, done more than scratch the surface. The progress has been wonderful enough but..."

Pages:300

Biographies/   **ISBN:** *1-59462-198-5*   *MSRP $21.95*

The Art of Cross-Examination
Francis Wellman

QTY

I presume it is the experience of every author, after his first book is published upon an important subject, to be almost overwhelmed with a wealth of ideas and illustrations which could readily have been included in his book, and which to his own mind, at least, seem to make a second edition inevitable. Such certainly was the case with me; and when the first edition had reached its sixth impression in five months, I rejoiced to learn that it seemed to my publishers that the book had met with a sufficiently favorable reception to justify a second and considerably enlarged edition. ..

Reference   **ISBN:** *1-59462-647-2*

Pages:412

MSRP $19.95

On the Duty of Civil Disobedience
Henry David Thoreau

QTY

Thoreau wrote his famous essay, On the Duty of Civil Disobedience, as a protest against an unjust but popular war and the immoral but popular institution of slave-owning. He did more than write—he declined to pay his taxes, and was hauled off to gaol in consequence. Who can say how much this refusal of his hastened the end of the war and of slavery ?

Law   **ISBN:** *1-59462-747-9*   **Pages:48**

MSRP $7.45

Dream Psychology Psychoanalysis for Beginners
Sigmund Freud

QTY

Sigmund Freud, born Sigismund Schlomo Freud (May 6, 1856 - September 23, 1939), was a Jewish-Austrian neurologist and psychiatrist who co-founded the psychoanalytic school of psychology. Freud is best known for his theories of the unconscious mind, especially involving the mechanism of repression; his redefinition of sexual desire as mobile and directed towards a wide variety of objects; and his therapeutic techniques, especially his understanding of transference in the therapeutic relationship and the presumed value of dreams as sources of insight into unconscious desires.

Pages:196

Psychology   **ISBN:** *1-59462-905-6*

MSRP $15.45

The Miracle of Right Thought
Orison Swett Marden

QTY

Believe with all of your heart that you will do what you were made to do. When the mind has once formed the habit of holding cheerful, happy, prosperous pictures, it will not be easy to form the opposite habit. It does not matter how improbable or how far away this realization may see, or how dark the prospects may be, if we visualize them as best we can, as vividly as possible, hold tenaciously to them and vigorously struggle to attain them, they will gradually become actualized, realized in the life. But a desire, a longing without endeavor, a yearning abandoned or held indifferently will vanish without realization.

Pages:360

Self Help   **ISBN:** *1-59462-644-8*

MSRP $25.45

QTY

The Rosicrucian Cosmo-Conception Mystic Christianity *by Max Heindel*　ISBN: *1-59462-188-8*　**$38.95**
The Rosicrucian Cosmo-conception is not dogmatic, neither does it appeal to any other authority than the reason of the student. It is: not controversial, but is: sent forth in the, hope that it may help to clear...　　　New Age/Religion Pages 646

Abandonment To Divine Providence *by Jean-Pierre de Caussade*　ISBN: *1-59462-228-0*　**$25.95**
"The Rev. Jean Pierre de Caussade was one of the most remarkable spiritual writers of the Society of Jesus in France in the 18th Century. His death took place at Toulouse in 1751. His works have gone through many editions and have been republished...　Inspirational/Religion Pages 400

Mental Chemistry *by Charles Haanel*　ISBN: *1-59462-192-6*　**$23.95**
Mental Chemistry allows the change of material conditions by combining and appropriately utilizing the power of the mind. Much like applied chemistry creates something new and unique out of careful combinations of chemicals the mastery of mental chemistry...　New Age Pages 354

The Letters of Robert Browning and Elizabeth Barret Barrett 1845-1846 vol II　ISBN: *1-59462-193-4*　**$35.95**
by Robert Browning and Elizabeth Barrett　　　Biographies Pages 596

Gleanings In Genesis (volume I) *by Arthur W. Pink*　ISBN: *1-59462-130-6*　**$27.45**
Appropriately has Genesis been termed "the seed plot of the Bible" for in it we have, in germ form, almost all of the great doctrines which are afterwards fully developed in the books of Scripture which follow...　Religion/Inspirational Pages 420

The Master Key *by L. W. de Laurence*　ISBN: *1-59462-001-6*　**$30.95**
In no branch of human knowledge has there been a more lively increase of the spirit of research during the past few years than in the study of Psychology, Concentration and Mental Discipline. The requests for authentic lessons in Thought Control, Mental Discipline and...　New Age/Business Pages 422

The Lesser Key Of Solomon Goetia *by L. W. de Laurence*　ISBN: *1-59462-092-X*　**$9.95**
This translation of the first book of the "Lernegton" which is now for the first time made accessible to students of Talismanic Magic was done, after careful collation and edition, from numerous Ancient Manuscripts in Hebrew, Latin, and French...　New Age/Occult Pages 92

Rubaiyat Of Omar Khayyam *by Edward Fitzgerald*　ISBN:*1-59462-332-5*　**$13.95**
Edward Fitzgerald, whom the world has already learned, in spite of his own efforts to remain within the shadow of anonymity, to look upon as one of the rarest poets of the century, was born at Bredfield, in Suffolk, on the 31st of March, 1809. He was the third son of John Purcell...　Music Pages 172

Ancient Law *by Henry Maine*　ISBN: *1-59462-128-4*　**$29.95**
The chief object of the following pages is to indicate some of the earliest ideas of mankind, as they are reflected in Ancient Law, and to point out the relation of those ideas to modern thought.　Religion/History Pages 452

Far-Away Stories *by William J. Locke*　ISBN: *1-59462-129-2*　**$19.45**
"Good wine needs no bush, but a collection of mixed vintages does. And this book is just such a collection. Some of the stories I do not want to remain buried for ever in the museum files of dead magazine-numbers an author's not unpardonable vanity..."　Fiction Pages 272

Life of David Crockett *by David Crockett*　ISBN: *1-59462-250-7*　**$27.45**
"Colonel David Crockett was one of the most remarkable men of the times in which he lived. Born in humble life, but gifted with a strong will, an indomitable courage, and unremitting perseverance...　Biographies/New Age Pages 424

Lip-Reading *by Edward Nitchie*　ISBN: *1-59462-206-X*　**$25.95**
Edward B. Nitchie, founder of the New York School for the Hard of Hearing, now the Nitchie School of Lip-Reading, Inc, wrote "LIP-READING Principles and Practice". The development and perfecting of this meritorious work on lip-reading was an undertaking...　How-to Pages 400

A Handbook of Suggestive Therapeutics, Applied Hypnotism, Psychic Science　ISBN: *1-59462-214-0*　**$24.95**
by Henry Munro　　　Health/New Age/Health/Self-help Pages 376

A Doll's House: and Two Other Plays *by Henrik Ibsen*　ISBN: *1-59462-112-8*　**$19.95**
Henrik Ibsen created this classic when in revolutionary 1848 Rome. Introducing some striking concepts in playwriting for the realist genre, this play has been studied the world over.　Fiction/Classics/Plays 308

The Light of Asia *by sir Edwin Arnold*　ISBN: *1-59462-204-3*　**$13.95**
In this poetic masterpiece, Edwin Arnold describes the life and teachings of Buddha. The man who was to become known as Buddha to the world was born as Prince Gautama of India but he rejected the worldly riches and abandoned the reigns of power when...　Religion/History/Biographies Pages 170

The Complete Works of Guy de Maupassant *by Guy de Maupassant*　ISBN: *1-59462-157-8*　**$16.95**
"For days and days, nights and nights, I had dreamed of that first kiss which was to consecrate our engagement, and I knew not on what spot I should put my lips..."　Fiction/Classics Pages 240

The Art of Cross-Examination *by Francis L. Wellman*　ISBN: *1-59462-309-0*　**$26.95**
Written by a renowned trial lawyer, Wellman imparts his experience and uses case studies to explain how to use psychology to extract desired information through questioning.　How-to/Science/Reference Pages 408

Answered or Unanswered? *by Louisa Vaughan*　ISBN: *1-59462-248-5*　**$10.95**
Miracles of Faith in China　　　Religion Pages 112

The Edinburgh Lectures on Mental Science (1909) *by Thomas*　ISBN: *1-59462-008-3*　**$11.95**
This book contains the substance of a course of lectures recently given by the writer in the Queen Street Hall, Edinburgh. Its purpose is to indicate the Natural Principles governing the relation between Mental Action and Material Conditions...　New Age/Psychology Pages 148

Ayesha *by H. Rider Haggard*　ISBN: *1-59462-301-5*　**$24.95**
Verily and indeed it is the unexpected that happens! Probably if there was one person upon the earth from whom the Editor of this, and of a certain previous history, did not expect to hear again...　Classics Pages 380

Ayala's Angel *by Anthony Trollope*　ISBN: *1-59462-352-X*　**$29.95**
The two girls were both pretty, but Lucy who was twenty-one who supposed to be simple and comparatively unattractive, whereas Ayala was credited, as her Bombwhat romantic name might show, with poetic charm and a taste for romance. Ayala when her father died was nineteen...　Fiction Pages 484

The American Commonwealth *by James Bryce*　ISBN: *1-59462-286-8*　**$34.45**
An interpretation of American democratic political theory. It examines political mechanics and society from the perspective of Scotsman James Bryce　Politics Pages 572

Stories of the Pilgrims *by Margaret P. Pumphrey*　ISBN: *1-59462-116-0*　**$17.95**
This book explores pilgrims religious oppression in England as well as their escape to Holland and eventual crossing to America on the Mayflower, and their early days in New England...　History Pages 268

QTY

The Fasting Cure by *Sinclair Upton* **ISBN: *1-59462-222-1* $13.95**
In the Cosmopolitan Magazine for May, 1910, and in the Contemporary Review (London) for April, 1910, I published an article dealing with my experiences in fasting. I have written a great many magazine articles, but never one which attracted so much attention... New Age/Self Help/Health Pages 164

Hebrew Astrology by *Sepharial* **ISBN: *1-59462-308-2* $13.45**
In these days of advanced thinking it is a matter of common observation that we have left many of the old landmarks behind and that we are now pressing forward to greater heights and to a wider horizon than that which represented the mind-content of our progenitors... Astrology Pages 144

Thought Vibration or The Law of Attraction in the Thought World **ISBN: *1-59462-127-6* $12.95**
by William Walker Atkinson *Psychology/Religion Pages 144*

Optimism by *Helen Keller* **ISBN: *1-59462-108-X* $15.95**
Helen Keller was blind, deaf, and mute since 19 months old, yet famously learned how to overcome these handicaps, communicate with the world, and spread her lectures promoting optimism. An inspiring read for everyone... Biographies/Inspirational Pages 84

Sara Crewe by *Frances Burnett* **ISBN: *1-59462-360-0* $9.45**
In the first place, Miss Minchin lived in London. Her home was a large, dull, tall one, in a large, dull square, where all the houses were alike, and all the sparrows were alike, and where all the door-knockers made the same heavy sound... Childrens/Classic Pages 88

The Autobiography of Benjamin Franklin by *Benjamin Franklin* **ISBN: *1-59462-135-7* $24.95**
The Autobiography of Benjamin Franklin has probably been more extensively read than any other American historical work, and no other book of its kind has had such ups and downs of fortune. Franklin lived for many years in England, where he was agent... Biographies/History Pages 332

Name	
Email	
Telephone	
Address	
City, State ZIP	

☐ **Credit Card**   ☐ **Check / Money Order**

Credit Card Number	
Expiration Date	
Signature	

Please Mail to: Book Jungle
PO Box 2226
Champaign, IL 61825
or Fax to: 630-214-0564

ORDERING INFORMATION

web: *www.bookjungle.com*
email: *sales@bookjungle.com*
fax: *630-214-0564*
mail: *Book Jungle PO Box 2226 Champaign, IL 61825*
or PayPal *to sales@bookjungle.com*

Please contact us for bulk discounts

DIRECT-ORDER TERMS

**20% Discount if You Order
Two or More Books**
Free Domestic Shipping!
Accepted: Master Card, Visa,
Discover, American Express